JAMES TINGLY AND THE CHEST OF THE AMAZON TRIBE

Sriramanathan Muralitharan

BLUEROSE PUBLISHERS
India | U.K.

Copyright © Sriramanathan Muralitharan 2023

All rights reserved by author. No part of this publication may be reproduced, stored in a retrieval system, or transmitted in any form or by any means, electronic, mechanical, photocopying, recording or otherwise, without the prior permission of the author. Although every precaution has been taken to verify the accuracy of the information contained herein, the publisher assumes no responsibility for any errors or omissions. No liability is assumed for damages that may result from the use of information contained within.

BlueRose Publishers takes no responsibility for any damages, losses, or liabilities that may arise from the use or misuse of the information, products, or services provided in this publication.

For permissions requests or inquiries regarding this publication, please contact:

BLUEROSE PUBLISHERS
www.BlueRoseONE.com
info@bluerosepublishers.com
+91 8882 898 898
+4407342408967

ISBN: 978-93-5819-295-7

Cover design: Shivam
Typesetting: Namrata Saini

First Edition: September 2023

To my beloved parents, lovely sister, and esteemed gurus.

Contents

The Characters 1

December Stress 3

Mayhem at the airport 8

Near disaster 15

The 'Inauspicious' flight 21

The reveal of the man 29

Masterpiece! 33

Uncrafting a paper 35

Loggia Amazonia! 41

The planning of the jungle heist 45

Who is that boy? 57

A disastrous truck goes into the forest! ... 63

That was 'inspiring' 69

The innovative bird hub! 71

The sloth bears 75

The jaguar saw us! 79

What just happened?	84
The Jaguar is hungry!	88
Well... Who do we have here?	90
Steve has arrived	92
The next 2 miles	95
The reveal of the imposter	105
Intelligent civilizations or foolish cannibals?	107
The gang is back!	113
The tribes turn good	117
The heist of our lives!	121
Back to Lodgia, Amazonia!	129
Back home!	134

The Characters

James Tingly Is the hero of this story. Or more likely, a jester in disguise.

Joe Tingly is the father of James Tingly. He is very fat because he got out of shape after his college days.

Mary Tingly, The mom of James She is very strict in her dining manners and house responsibilities.

Thomas Rex: The proud travel guide of the Amazon Jungle resorts He has earned the world record for the 'longest survivor in a forest'.

Preston Von Smith: The international criminal! He is known for smuggling rare wood to Africa.

Jingle Jonga: The King of the Forest He is bulky, speaks his own language, and always has a blowpipe with snake venom in it for punishing others or for a quick getaway.

December Stress

I went to school for the last day and had some hot chocolate for free in the canteen. Yes, they give everyone in school free burgers and French fries at the end of the semester. But I quit both of them because the burger was cold as ice and I couldn't even bite through it. And the cheese was rock solid. And the French fries were soaking wet. They were still hot. But I wasn't taking any chances because I heard rumours that the school's cleaner was the only chef who knew how to fry French fries. And when I saw him taking the French fries with his bare hands like a bulldozer, I felt my stomach flip-flop. So, I didn't even make eye contact with the fries. The hot chocolate was the only thing I could muster, but believe me, if the cleaner had it in his hands, I would have flushed the chocolate down the drain. They also hand out fruit juice for the sake of our "developing brain." But the bucket in which they pour was something very familiar, and when my mind caught up to it, I excused myself and ran up to the bathroom and stayed there until this whole end-of-the-year "party" was over. Man, our school should read about some hygiene! Not only that, all the boys and girls in our school, even after knowing this dark truth, were hogging down their fill and, even worse, slurping every last bit of their food. But I did not have to see the whole scene, or things might have gone out of hand, or, should I say, out of my mouth. Well, one boy named George McMalan went to the nurse's office saying he had a stomach-ache, and actually, half of the school followed him, and when I say half, I mean that in my class, only 7 students were there, including me. Well, if this means 'God is watching, I will be its advocate. Well, the school had to shut down, and my dad wasn't happy to get a call when he was on Movie Day Friday. After I went home,

I heard my mom call out, and I went down. She said we needed to start decorating the house right now because Christmas was due in three days. But I said there were no decorating things in our house for now. So, she said to take my bike and ride to the department store, which is three houses ahead. I took my jacket and my cap and pedalled away to the store. But I think I was speeding because when I put on the brakes, I went sliding on the road and crashed on the fence of Randy Fedro's house. Well, Randy's dad wasn't happy to see his fence broken, so I made a run for my money. But I was disappointed to see the store closed. So, I went home, and this time, I was going way slower than a sloth. When I reached home, I told my mom that the store was closed. Just then, my dad came in his car and said that all the stores were closed. My mom said that we needed to drive to Walmart, but my dad said that Walmart was 40 km away and he did not want to waste his time. Walmart's actually cool, but seeing the price for a small candy cane last year, I lost interest in it. My mom and dad started arguing, and before this blew out into a family burst, I went upstairs. You know, there is only so much a person can take. Upstairs, I thought about this thing. This year, my Wishlist is huge, and the house looks like it was hit by a tornado. And with this scenario, the mom and dad family war is going on, and the house might look like it was demolished. And if Santa trips on anything when he walks into our house at night, I am not the boy to blame. After 2 hours or so, there was silence below. I went down, and then I saw Mom packing her suitcase as well as dad. Then Mom came down and said we were going to this resort in the Amazon Forest, and we were going to celebrate our Christmas there. It was -11 degrees Celsius out there, and the weather report said that it was going to snow like crazy today. But actually, I am happy with things like this, and I don't care about others, but I stay in my house, light the fire, sit on the couch with a cup of hot chocolate, and hog it myself watching Christmas specials on TV. But this trip was something tropical and wild. My mom said to pack my bags. I was about to ask why we should go there, but dad made the case harder because he was done and ready for the trip and he wore an outfit that was meant for tropical regions, but it was snowing out there, and at -11 degrees Celsius, my dad would be frozen solid. Well, my mom was on this trip, and I wouldn't argue anymore. I took my suitcase, packed my bags, and got ready for the trip.

Mayhem at the airport

My dad saw all the bookings available, and he said almost all the flights were booked for Christmas. That meant our trip had a chance to come to an end. I was kind of enjoying this, but dad landed the axe the next moment. He said that there is only one flight available, and that is for tomorrow. It had three seats. Well, I don't, but happiness never likes me. Tonight, we did not have any supplies because dad ate all the snacks in the fridge for his Movie Day Friday and all the supplies were used up for lunch. So, we had to manage with leftovers from lunch. After that small nibble, I went over to the bed. But my stomach was so hurt that the only cure was FOOD. dad told me that I had to wake up very early, so I slept at 9:00. But I couldn't sleep anymore because, at midnight, I was shivering and had a feeling that my toe had been paralysed. Well, the heater was not running in my room. I went near it. It was silent. So, I went down to dad's room, and the heater was not running there either. I went to the living room, and it was dead there too. I woke up dad, who had icicles hanging from his mouth, and he went down to the basement. I didn't take any chances because the basement is also one of my worst fears. I heard dad calling from underneath, so I took a deep breath and went down. dad said the boiler had run out of wood. Our house is one of those houses that still uses old-school stuff like this boiler. Other people in our neighbourhood had electric boilers, so all of them were in their dreamworld by now. I went up to the attic where we kept all the wood, and as I expected, there was no wood in the rack. When I went back to the basement, I heard upstairs who didn't like to be awake at 1:00. My dad said we had to manage this day and the next day; we would sort it out at the airport. But I didn't have a good night's sleep because I think the temperature had dropped by -2 and there was a snowstorm outside at 3:00 at midnight. I would have traded my room for Randy's cowshed. But I didn't know how, but I finally slept at... well, I don't know, but I heard my dad waking me up at 5:30 in the morning, and my stomach was shrivelled up and my ribs were visible very clearly. I didn't have the energy to wake up. I still needed some brain rest to keep my motors going. But dad wasn't gambling, and he said the flight was due at 7:30! I got up, brushed my teeth, and when I went to the bathroom, that's where things started getting wrong. Do you remember when the boiler stopped working because there was no wood left? Well, when I said old school, I literally meant OLD SCHOOL because this whole house needed this one boiler for heat, and the water too was heated this way, and as the boiler was not working, the water came out freezing cold. I didn't want to take a bath, but my mom said I should. And when I smelled my body, I was practically dead, and it was all thanks to yesterday's end-of-the-year party. I forgot to mention that yesterday, the cleaner was serving the juice, and when he came to pour some into my glass, I refused right in the nick of time, and in that shock, he spilled some of the juice in my shirt. But when I came home, I don't know how, but I completely forgot that incident, and my body was smelling like garbage. At that moment, I learned one lesson. If you ever get yourself drenched in juice served in garbage cans, and even if you had to bathe in ice in Antarctica, you will have to, because if you smelled yourself one day, you would have jumped in the ice in a heartbeat. After that shower, my legs felt like they would fall off because I was shivering from the cold. I didn't have much of a shower either because after some time, the water stopped coming out, and I think the water froze, so I gave up. But I was ready! dad said he had booked a taxi, and it would be there in 15 minutes. But that's where something very nasty happened. I took a step forward, but my legs were shivering with the cold, and I stubbed my leg on the hinge of the door, and that's it; I was jumping up between the sky and the Earth. My toe was bleeding. My mom took the first aid box and quickly bandaged my injury. But I couldn't take a step. My dad looked pretty crossed because the flight must have cost a lot, especially when you book it at the last second. And just at that time, the taxi reached our house. It was such perfect timing because my toe was throbbing, and seeing the taxi, my dad started jumping too. Mom told me that we could take a wheelchair from the airport. My dad loaded the suitcase in the boot, and we got going. After some time, though, things started getting lousy. There was a traffic jam on the way. That was so frustrating. And I think the truck driver and the bike driver in front of us were thinking the same because he banged the truck to his right, and the truck driver came out to let the bike driver know, and before you knew it, the two of them got themselves into an all-out fight. This made us even madder, and I think the families behind us were thinking the same. I think one of the families called the cops because two cops came in on their motorcycles, and both were busted. But my dad was more worried about the time because our flight was due in another 30 minutes! Luckily, after the two of them were caught by the cops, the traffic started moving pretty fast, and the taxi driver took off. I think he was hearing Rocketman in his earphones because, after the traffic, it was just 5th gear. At a certain point, he did put the pedal to the metal. We had almost reached the airport, but the driver must have realised there was a mini-toll gate right in front of him, so he put the brakes on so hard, and that sent the car into a drift. We lost the lane to the toll gate for cars, and we drifted into the toll gate of the shuttle bus. But the car was smoking, and it was still going at 80 kilometres per hour, so we were pretty much done. The toll gate was closed, and we went full speed towards it.

Near disaster

I closed my eyes, and my dad was shouting to put on the brakes, and my mom was squelching like an opera singer. But after that, I heard a slight thud. I thought I had reached my destination, Heaven, but to my surprise, the taxi had made it alive, and it just made a slight thud on the pavement. My dad said that the toll gate was a bit too high, and the taxi went underneath the toll gate. I think the scene was pretty ironic because people started gathering near the spot. We didn't have anything to do there, so we ran away, hiding our faces. But somehow, we escaped that near-death incident. We reached the airport, but then I felt something was missing, and it was my luggage! I told dad that I had not taken my luggage from the taxi. dad said he would go and get our luggage and said we should continue going to the airport. We went into the airport, which was huge, and my eyes were painful. It was almost like the whole thing was made of ivory because you couldn't see it without sunglasses. This was the first time I had ever been on a flight. If I had known that the airport was like this, I would not have been on this trip. Mom tagged along with me. We went to the ticket counter and met with the recipient. Mom showed us the ticket for our flight, and the recipient approved it and showed us the way to our terminal. We still had 20 minutes. So, we could make it. But mom made a stop and said that apparently, dad had taken all of our luggage to get mine, so we should wait till we get our luggage because they would ask for our luggage for checking. I felt lucky because if Mom had taken me into the crowd, I would have been squished to death. We waited and waited until we had only 10 minutes in hand. Mom made a phone call, and dad said He was walking towards the airport. He said that there was a shuttle bus, but he had missed it, and the next bus would take another hour. So he was running towards the airport. He told us to move through the ticket counter because they would let us go without luggage too. We stood in the line, and man, was it a line! Christmas is one of the busiest festivals of the year, and I am learning about it now. But luckily, everyone was a bit formal, so they stood with a gap. This was good manners. Now I didn't have any problems standing, and there wasn't any touching and shoving or things like that. But the line seemed like it didn't move at all. Everyone in the line seemed to be in the mood for some tropical fun. I heard one of the cops beside me say that one of the conveyors was damaged, the other conveyor didn't have an operator, and the new guy operating it was a noob, letting only one passenger go every 10 minutes. That meant we didn't have a chance. I wanted this to go on, and there were only 2 minutes left. dad was on the other side of the line, and he waved his hands at us. He said to come there, but with 50 people behind us, it wasn't going to be easy. But the line at which dad was standing was moving fast, and our line was moving a bit faster than before. I think the new guy operating the conveyor really got the hang of it. And man, this was luck on its next level; just as we made it to the front of the line, dad was also in the front of the line, and we had our bags checked at the same time. We made it, and dad tagged along with us. The people who were standing in the line weren't crushing everyone and had made gaps. But the humidity with all those people in the line was humongous, and I was sweating from head to toe. Thinking of my toes, I remembered that my toe pain was gone. We had gotten out of the line, but it seemed pretty much doomed at that point because we had only one minute left and we needed to run all the way to the end of the airport to get to our gate. There were a total of 33 gates in the airport, and our gate was gate 8, which was on the same floor as us. That was luck in our hands. The experience wasn't great. And my suitcase was very old. And when I say old, we are speaking of 82 years now. The suitcase that I had was from great-grandma Bethrine, and my dad had kept this suitcase as her sentiment. When I was born, I was allowed to keep this suitcase. But my dad never let me oil the wheels because he wanted them to remain untouched and just as they were. So now that I am running, the rusted wheel is pulling me the other way. Luckily, there was this vehicle like a boogie bike, and we hopped on it for a ride. I should have had a second thought because the driver was another replacement staff member and he seemed new to the job, just like the conveyor belt operator. He put the pedal to the metal. He was going so fast that the taxi driver made me feel better. He almost crashed through the crowd, but the brakes were pretty strong, so we drifted on the carpet. But the ride was worth it, and the special part is that this ride was FREE. Now we just needed to enter our terminal, but we had gone way past our time. But dad said we had luck because some flights let the door open for some of the last-minute passengers. Then there was a call, and this was the call we were waiting for: "Any passengers travelling to Brazil, this is the final call!" So, we were on our heels again, and right before they closed the aerobridge, we had dived into the door and shown the air hostess our tickets. We went into the aerobridge, and man, that run had really had my legs throbbing. I think we ran a lot, so maybe my dad also lost some weight. But we made it through.

The 'Inauspicious' flight

We entered the plane, and it wasn't even great. The seats were so small that even children like me would have to be packed in. It was completely covered in leather, though, which made it a bit comfy. It was so tempting to see that I plopped into one of the seats and instantly fell asleep! Unusual for a small flight like this. The height of the flight was small, too. And from the outside, this plane model looked like one from the late 1970s, and it didn't have any engines. Instead, it had these huge propellers, and I don't think that is aerodynamic at all. So, there must be a lot of turbulence. Each side has three seats, and that made the aisle so small. But dad was sitting on the other side. He said someone else booked the seat. I think they were the last passengers. But some guy made it in at the last second, and I wasn't even hazed. He wore a brown coat with a cowboy hat on his head, and he had all these things in his pockets. He came in and sat beside us. Mom said to shift places because she didn't want to sit there. I switched seats with her, but I got to know why. That man seems to have never bathed in his life. And if he is a regular passenger on this plane, then no doubt the seats smell so bad. But mom was pretty sneaky, and she ditched me in this trap. But it was too late, and I had to spend like 8 hours sitting near this guy. I looked at dad, and there was no one besides him. His rights and lefts were empty, and he had the best luck while I was stuck with this guy who looks like he was directly imported from Man vs. Wild. But it wasn't just his smell. It was all these spikes he had in his boots and all the pocketknives in his coat. I don't know how they let this man on the flight, but something told me he was not here for the flight and was here for some... you know, terrorism or something? I don't know, but if he was, I should keep my stuff ready because I would take a parachute bag and go skydive if I were in this situation. The flight actually took off, and I was pretty nervous at the point where it raised. The seatbelt lights went on, and I put them on. But no one on the flight cared, and I wasn't going to let them go like that. I didn't have much to do, so I thought of eating some snacks. It was in my suitcase, but it wasn't there. I informed Mom, and she said she didn't see me with it when I entered the flight. That's when I remembered that I felt my hands released in first class. I waited for some time, and when the pilot informed us we had reached cruising altitude and also when the seatbelt lights went off, I went to the first-class coach, but there was a flight attendant there, and she said people in economy class were not allowed in first-class. I informed her that my suitcase was there and also added an extra bit that my dad was there, and she let me in. I went there and searched all the places in first class. Some people even asked what I was doing here and why I was looking troubled. But no one had even seen my suitcase. I asked the air hostess, and she said she had seen one rusty suitcase, and it was too big to put in the flight, so she had ditched it under the flight. Now that was bad. They didn't even ask whose suitcase it was. But the snacks were in the suitcase, and now they are on the flight. That was pretty bad. I went to sit in my seat, and this man had slept in his seat, and I could see his legs going to the armrest of my seat. Now I had his dirty shoes pointing right in my face, and not only that, but his shoes also had spikes. So, if I had sat there, then I would have had someone breathing under my throat. The only way I could go to my seat was in two ways:

1. Crawling under the man
2. Jumping over the man

I wasn't really skilled in either of these, but I thought that jumping would be really cool.

But you know, it's not easy to jump over a man who is 7 feet tall. So, I crawled under him, but it was the wrong idea because his pants seemed to stick to him from when he was born. But the pants weren't the only problem. It was the belt. The spikes were almost 4 inches tall, and I could feel the cold iron spikes rubbing my spine when I crawled beneath him. That wasn't the greatest feeling because even if you nudged a little, the spikes would pierce your back. But I made it somehow, and now his legs were in my seat. He had luckily put on his shoes because if he had opened them, I don't know, but the shoes must have corroded. And there were still 7 hours of flight left, and I don't know when he will wake up. So, as soon as I made it, I crawled back to the aisle, and again, I was pinched with the spikes. I went to dad's seat, but he was way worse than that man there, and he had occupied the three seats completely for himself. So, he was paying for only one seat and using two free seats, and he had comfort like in sleeper class, and seeing him made me quite jealous. He was having a peaceful time while I was stuck with this guy who seemed to be a killer! So the better deal was this: I had to go somewhere to spend my time. I heard we can bargain with some passengers and change our seats. But when I looked at them, they didn't seem in the mood to talk. They were giving me the red eye, which people mostly give on Halloween. But then I saw something that was like gold. It was the food trolley. It was used to deliver food to the passengers, but it was 10:00 in the morning and no one was in the mood to eat brunch. I guess that's good because I can use the trolley as my seat. But if anyone asks for food, then I am dead. So I slept in the cabinet underneath. It was actually a bit more comfortable than the seats because it was covered with velvet, and it felt like I was sleeping in a grassland. I slept on it, and I didn't know time was passing by. But after an hour or so, I heard some creaking, and when I woke up completely, I felt I was moving. That's when it struck me. My worst fears were coming true! Someone was using the trolley! And when I looked at the time, it was 1:00 p.m., and it seemed everyone was in the mood for lunch. Luckily, there was this cloth that covered the cabinet, and I was undercover. I had an idea. I was pretty good at sneaking up on others, and if I had a little peek at what was outside, I could get to know my seat, and when they made a pit stop there, I could secretly jump out and sit in my place. I pulled up the cloth a tiny bit just to allow my eyes to see everyone's boots. But I think I should not have done that because, soon, I smelled something funny, and I knew exactly where I was. I pulled up the cloth a little bit for a peek, and I saw a boot covered with spikes. I jumped out and quickly wriggled under that man's legs, and I jumped to my seat. That guy didn't even seem to notice that. The air hostess asked what he wanted, and he told her to bring some toad meat, which was pretty disgusting. The air hostess looked disgusted and said there was only mutton gravy and chicken fries in non-veg, and that man seemed to be drooling. He ordered a chicken fry, and I ordered some sandwiches and bacon. It was enough for me. Considering the smell of the man, I think I might throw up for this small quantity of food. I was pretty relieved that the man went to the bathroom. I didn't know he was really hygienic enough to wash his hands. But he came out as soon as he came in, and I knew I wasn't taking any chances.

The reveal of the man

I never knew the food on the flight would be so good because it was nothing like what I have eaten at home and in restaurants. But the man came right beside me, and I lost my appetite. I really became fed up with this 'man, and I decided to speak up and show him who I was. But right when I opened my mouth, the man started speaking with me! He asked, "What is up, little fella'? The food's bad here, isn't it?" I didn't know what to say. I was stunned for a second. Then I spoke up. I said, "I am James Tingly, and I live in Massachusetts." After that, the man spoke about himself. He started introducing himself. "My name is Thomas Rex. I am a forest expert and the Guinness World Record holder for the longest survivor in a wild forest without facilities. I work as a travel guide in the Loggia Amazonia." When I heard where he worked, I was pretty impressed. And I got answers to why he was dirty and why he had all those knives and stuff. But one thing was unclear. What was he doing on the flight? I asked him, and he said he had come there to stop a wild puma in the zoo. That did seem so confusing. It isn't like I know a lot of General Knowledge these days. The flight was still due to land. The flight would land in another hour. I had a small conversation with that guy because he really seems to be one of the guys on the Discovery Channel, and I really don't know why such a celebrity would be here in economy class. Maybe his smell wasn't good for first class, or maybe his salary was yet to be negotiated. But that wasn't my business. But after some time, there was a shake and a very bad sound. As soon as I felt the jerk, I jumped and stood in my seat. I thought of running towards the door, but then the pilot came upon the speakers and made an excuse, saying it was turbulence. I wasn't going to take that because, in a second, the plane might be sunk under the ocean. But it was a steady flight after that, and at 7:45 p.m., we reached the destination. I didn't know what was happening for some time because I had slept soundly, and don't even ask me how. But when I felt the heat on my cheeks, I had a very nice feeling. It had a tropical feel. We had landed in a very great place. The airport was cool. But it still wasn't completed. We had to drive to a spot in the Amazon Forest, and our resort was there. The shuttle bus arrived, and I climbed into it. I took my suitcase, and we went in search of a taxi. But this time, we booked the airport taxi and made sure the car was speed monitored. The rest of the ride was into the woods, and it was really damp and wet. The driver said it was dangerous out here. That wasn't the best first impression, but he went on. He said that the animals we need to look out for are jaguars, ocelots, mosquitoes, wasps, howler monkeys, anacondas, jaguars, green vipers, and a lot more. I was taking notes of all he said because I didn't want to end this trip as dead meat for jaguars. After that, I was sound asleep when I was woken up by a small vibration. I noticed we had left the road and were going on the 'rough and tough' side. This taxi, though, had a larger ground clearance. We reached the resort, but it didn't have any rooms on first impression. The gates opened and the Jeep climbed in, and we turned right to witness an absolute

Masterpiece!

It was a hut—an actual hut! I am not saying this in anger, but in happiness. You know one of the activities on my wish list was to stay in a real hut for at least one day, and I am really glad it is coming true before the year ends. The jeep stopped, and the driver said the dinner was buffet and we had to check in at the reception. The reception was also a hut, but inside, things looked quite teak and neat! We checked in, and some guys with white dresses and gloves carried our luggage, and we walked to our room, which was also a hut. It also had a hammock outside and a swing, which was actually a rubber tyre tied to a tree. This was one of the best moments of my life. I mean, it is not so frequent that you get to see a high-tech hut. My dad slipped a card into the door, and it opened. I went inside, and it wasn't so fancy, but it was okay for being a hut on the outside. It had two beds and one bathroom. But the biggest disappointment was that there was no TV! There was a book at the side, and it was about the forest. Apparently, they said there was no internet connection or any frequencies in the forest because it might harm the beautiful birds. It was night, and there hadn't been anything to do for a long time. I just spied a small nightstand in the corner, and I wondered what was in it. I slid it open, and I saw a few crunchy snacks. I didn't take that seriously because they were barbecue-flavoured, which I hated. But when I closed it, there was a big knock on it. I opened the slab on the nightstand once again, and I saw the same thing. But that's when I mistakenly knocked over my dad's charger, and I bent down to pick it up. That's when I saw the nightstand was only half opened, and I tried to pull the slab a bit further, but it didn't budge. I didn't know what to do. I tried pulling it once again, and the slab creaked open, and what I saw there shocked me.

Uncrafting a paper

I saw a small pocket chest, and it was covered with watery soil. I took it, and the wet soil started dripping on the floor. It was very strange, and I wasn't ready to open it just YET. I wasn't sure what was inside. So, I gave it a small rattle, and there was a sound of something hard banging on it. I went into the bathroom and gave it a wash. It was very perplexing. The images on the chest seemed really old, and some were really disturbing. One of the pictures showed a ghost-like face ripping a human in half, and other people were running away. There were some animals etched in it too, and they were just some fantastical beasts. Like, would you really believe there were animals that were half chicken and half snake? Now that I know what is outside, I am actually trembling to know what is inside. But still, I gathered some courage and kept it in my bed to open it. It lay there, and I was on the other side, my trembling hands reaching for it. I was sure there was going to be a blast. I slowly took it in. I grasped it really tight. There was a small latch, and I opened it. This was the moment I slowly opened to have a peak. It was dark, and I couldn't see anything in the chest. I just gave up and completely opened it, and there was chocolate. Actually, nothing seemed synced these days. Last time, when Jake sent me into time, I saw a red button that told me to stay alert, and then there was this word written below it called 'Shrink, which didn't seem synced at all, and I almost got shrunk in the time machine. And now there is this chest that has all these gruesome sculptures etched in it, and when you open it, there is this sweet, small chocolate. I took it, and I noticed this chocolate was actually like nothing I had ever eaten before. I turned it around, and it had this written: Mfg. date: 3/6/1972

Eat by date: 6/18/1972

So, the chocolate was really old. I think it was about the time my father was born. I was really dejected. So, I threw it in front of me; it hit the wall and fell down, and there were these writings on it: 'Open at once, Dumbhead!' If anyone bought this, he really wanted us to eat it. But it has expired by now, and there is no way anyone can take a bite. If it expired one day ago, you could have it, but this thing expired years ago, and I couldn't even let my mind imagine just how the chocolate would be looking or smelling! Seeing the words, I really got my head scratching. So, I took the chocolate and ripped the wrapper in one go without thinking of what to do next, and there weren't any chocolate bars in it; it was a giant piece of paper folded in it! It looked very old because the edges were coming out like threads and the paper was really rough and yellow. I took the paper and unfolded it slowly, taking care not to tear anything. When there was only one fold to go, I got really curious. dad and Mom were outside having a stroll in the park. I was here alone in my room. Could things get any better? I slowly unfolded the last bit, and there was this huge blast of sparks, and a beam of light blinded me! All of a sudden, there was a chain reaction, and that piece of paper was floating in the air. I was startled by this sudden explosion. The map slowly came down and fell on my hands. I took a hold of it, and I saw what it was. It had this written on it: The map of the great Hound Hog tribes, and below it, there was a huge map. There was a line starting from somewhere near the sea and ending at a place that looked like a forest, and there was a short, funny-looking guy there. I was kind of perplexed by what I was seeing. "Holy Amazon, this thing is fantastical!" I said to myself. This map seemed very old. In fact, I am pretty sure that some parts of the map faded away. I really am ready for an adventure. I mean, after everything that happened when I went through time, a small booby trap isn't even a thing to me. Maybe I am pushing my confidence too far. So I headed out to see dad. I got up with dad halfway through the pavement, and I whispered in his ears, "I have something to show you in private," and dad seemed to get a general idea. At the suite, dad diverted Mom to the restaurant to see if the buffet was ready to eat. While she was out, I showed dad the map. He took it really carefully and examined it. He kept it really close to his eyes, and suddenly, there was a spark of colour in his eyes. It seemed to bulge out, and suddenly there was an explosion! "It is the great map created by the explorer Gusteer Rex! Man, he was one of the biggest explorers and celebrities of his time! He had a huge fan base, you know," my dad narrated. "But what exactly is the map saying?" I asked. My dad shrugged. You know, I am still not in 9th grade enough to know how to decode maps and stuff. I think dad flunked the classes anyway because he had told me that he would be in the theatres watching action movies during his schooling. So, we needed a real forest expert who could decode this map. Then it stroked me.

Loggia Amazonia!

I asked dad, "Do you know the name of this resort?" dad seemed slightly confused. He said he had read something like Lodge, Amazon, and things like that. I quickly searched for the book, and it had this name on it.

Travel Guide

Loggia Amazonia

This is it! This is the place! It is the Loggia Amazonia. The place where Thomas Rex is a travel guide I kept the map in the same box. I took it and ran as fast as my feet could carry me. "Wait for me!" dad shouted, but now he was far behind. I ran to the reception, banged on the table, and asked "Can I see the travel guide, Thomas Rex?" and I collapsed on the chair. The receptionist seemed shocked by fear, and he jumped and ran to a big room opposite the reception. Two seconds later, I heard thumping footsteps, and in front of me, there was the great man, Thomas Rex! "What is it, boy? Was it a Leopard? An Anaconda? Tell me, boy, what was it? dad came rolling and panting to the spot. "It was... the maf... the MAF..." and dad collapsed on the chair beside me. Well, that was the highest torque my dad could muster. "What is he telling me, son?" Rex asked me. "It is about the great map!" I replied. "What map?" asked Rex, who seemed to tremble a bit. But I would take that as a sign of being alert. Then I explained everything that happened in the hotel room to the box and the map. "The map was very old." I insisted. When I turned my head up, I saw Thomas Rex's eyes tearing up! "What's the matter?" dad piped in. "Gusteer Rex was my granddad!" Rex said it emotionally. "He died because of a Howler monkey." I giggled. I mean, it isn't so often you hear about someone dying because of howler monkey attacks. But Rex roared suddenly. "I will find this unauspicious place on behalf of my dad!". Well, that was dramatic. dad told me the plan. "Tomorrow is the jungle safari. We will pretend to come in a different van and start our trek into the woods." Rex said some of the tracks were going straight into the enclosures of some animals. So, we had to take some gear. Luckily, the resort had some licenced double barrels and crossbows in case of any animal emergencies. So, we could use them for our forest break-in. I wasn't really brave about this adventure. I am a guy who likes staying cosy at home. Just thinking about going into the animal enclosure was freaking me out, and I didn't want to end up with a skeleton to be found centuries later. Luckily, dad came to my aid. "James is too small to get into the woods. So James should stay here," dad said. "Sir, we really need James because he was the one who found the map!" Rex said. I was confused. "Why does that matter for anything?" I asked, trembling. "Look at this! The little text here!" Rex said, handing me a magnifying glass. The paper was a bit yellow, so I couldn't really see most of the text on the map. Most of them faded away. When I got a closer look at the text, I froze and turned pale with fear. Do you know why? This is what it said on the map.

The planning of the jungle heist

I wailed. This whole map was a trap! I knew the box was a bit suspicious. "We should leave for the woods immediately tomorrow morning. This map's a serious danger, and it could land us in peril." Rex insisted with a really serious tone and a lot of his spit flying out. I was still wailing. Why, oh why, should I have found that box in the first place? Many people would have been at the resort. Why didn't they pick it up before I got my hands on this rotten stuff? Mom passed by, and I quickly rubbed my face. Mom said with excitement, "The buffet is ready, and it is barbeque style! We better get going to get the best food soon!" We said goodbye to Rex and made our way to the buffet. After a hearty meal, we went to our room. But I couldn't sleep the whole night because I was very terrified. Who knows what monsters may be lurking in the woods? I think I slept at about 3:00, but I woke up because I felt something biting my thigh, and when I saw what it was, I toppled over the edge of the bed. It was a swarm of bed bugs! I went into the bathroom and plopped into the bucket of water, but it was unimaginably cold! I felt like I froze, and so did the bed bugs. They became stiff and sank to the bottom of the bucket. I came back to the room. I felt very cold. I thought it must be humid outside. So I opened the door, and the breeze made me feel even colder. This forest was especially cold at night. I think it must have reached zero! The bed was just useless now because the bed bugs had arranged a whole clan there, and they seemed to have a lot of fun. I, on the other hand, was shivering so much that my eyes must have popped out! In this decent room, there wasn't even a towel to dry me off. I gave up after that, and I slept on the floor by making a blanket out of my shirts. I think all the other guys back in Massachusetts may be having a blast celebrating Christmas and watching Christmas specials on TV while I am stuck in this jungle with creepy crawlies all over the place. After this whole mayhem, it was 3:30, and I didn't know if I could get some sleep. I was cold and stiff. At the same time, I was also fearing that I might die due to the curse or that a leopard would devour my head. I managed to slip off to sleep, but I woke up again. I don't know when, but it was pretty dark outside. This time, I felt something crawling over me. I opened my eyes just to come face to face with a really, really massive spider, and this one was orange and black like a tiger. I shrieked at once and jumped up until I hit the tiled roof. Then I fell on the linoleum floor and broke my knee. But I jumped again and started waving my hands like crazy. I was invaded by a tiger spider! It did not let go. I think the racket I created was enough for dad and mom to wake up, and as soon as dad saw me, he shrieked just like me and kicked off into the closet and locked himself in it. I think it was all the MOMs who, in this case, locked themselves into the closets while seeing a spider. But not my mom. She has mastered karate and Tai-chi, and she is the exterminator of my house, or rather, HER house. She jumped, did a somersault, and landed like Spider-Man on the floor. She quickly did a barrel roll and took the broom, and she quickly whacked me to the ground. The spider was squished, and its gooey juice splattered on my dress. I think that is the end of that spider, and I am good with my older shirts. So, I quickly threw my shirt in disgust and put on a new shirt. dad came out of the closet after 2 minutes or so. Mom just shot him a look and went back to sleep. We were pretty much awake at 4:46, so we were getting ready for the Jungle Safari. It was after the breakfast buffet. Thinking of going into the woods completely hopeless is really terrifying. Even if there is a bus with cages and high-tech safety, you really can't tell when a leopard will pounce on it and bite off the tyres. But me, dad, and Rex are going into the woods even without a mere sense of protection because everyone is fascinated with this treasure thing. I am so shaken up that now I doubt that the crossbow would even cause the slightest injury to a jaguar. What if the crossbow didn't work? What if the string breaks? What if the arrows were blunt? Or what if we missed the Jaguar? My mind was filled with all these catastrophic scenarios. It may be the end of me. It was 7:00 in the morning, and someone knocked on the door. dad went ahead and opened the door, and I could see Rex standing there. I quickly hid under the bed. I really didn't want to see him right now. From under the bed, I could hear some of the conversations. "Sir, we have a nature walk camp, sir. It is just now. If you are interested in joining, you can." I heard Rex's voice. For 3 seconds, a sinister silence fell, and then I heard the door close. I waited there for 2 seconds and then came out. dad quickly grabbed me by my shoulder and said, "Son, quickly get ready." He whispered in my ear, and then he woke up Mom and said, "Me and James are going for a nature walk. You wait right here and get prepared for the Safari." and then he put on his coat and mufflers and went out. So, I quickly put on a jacket and rushed after dad. It wasn't too cold or too hot. It was the perfect temperature. But I knew it was a subject that was going to change because, in the afternoon, it would become incredibly humid and hot. Luckily, I got a pair of SPF 30 sunscreens. We walked on the rock pavement and entered the reception, where we saw Rex. He was really into the map. When he saw us, he just gestured for us to come in. We sat nearby so that we could get a good look at the map. It looked as if Rex's eyes were drooping. It was early in the morning, and I hadn't had my coffee yet. So, I quickly poured some coffee into a cup from the nearby coffee machine. When I stepped inside, Rex started with a sad voice, "Guys, I don't think it is any use to go to the treasure." I had just taken a huge gulp of coffee, and those words gave me such a terrible shock that I spit out the whole lot. "WHAT ARE YOU SAYING?! I AM ABOUT TO DIE FOR FINDING THIS MAP. IF I DO NOT GO THERE, I AM DEAD! I AM CEMETRY!" I exclaimed, breathing like a bull after chasing a matador. "You see, James, even if you are taking this path, you die. It is full of BOOBY TRAPS! By the way, the treasure seems to be unworthy because it has only about two hundred thousand dollars of gold, which is a very small amount!" I was shocked. "MY WHOLE LIFE DEPENDS ON IT! YOU WERE THE ONE WHO SAID THAT THIS THING WAS CURSED, AND NOW YOU SAY IT IS UNWORTHY! I WILL GO TO THAT TREASURE!" I screamed at the top of my lungs, and it caught the attention of two guys strolling to the restaurant. They stared at me. I stared at them back. Before they could ask us about the treasure, my dad quickly sprang into action. "But this game costs 120 bucks, and I am not paying them! By the way, who would want a wacko treasure hunt game? Play Mario Bros! One of the most popular modern games!" dad said. I was quite confused for a second, but I understood the whole scene. dad was trying to cover up the treasure hunt I was talking about. So I quickly responded, "Mario Bros. is out of date!" TREASURE PIRATES ARE SO COOL! BUY ME A TREASURE PIRATE GAME!" The two guys shrugged at each other and continued down the pavement, disappearing into the thick morning fog. "JAMES, do you have any SENSE?! This whole mission is highly confidential. We have only two hundred dollars, and we have to split that into two more shares! If others dive in, then we would be doomed!" My dad said Well, well.

These days, everyone is behind this green piece of paper called "a bill". I didn't reply to anything because dad is already a money person. Suddenly, a mechanic called out for Rex, saying, "Sir, the Jeep's ready! We can go rough and tough after breakfast. She ain't quitting this time. She would go for a long time. I had it repaired again". "Make sure that her brakes are good. This is a serious issue, man! Did you have an oil check?" Rex asked. "I sure did! I think I did. But anyway, looking at her state, I think she could make it this time," the mechanic replied. He had a funny Texas accent when he spoke, and he always shot some spit. But what really mattered was the phrase 'She could make it this time' said by that mechanic. What did he mean when he said it this time? First of all, we are in a place in Brazil, and we have a guy from Texas. I know that a horse can't run all the way to Brazil from Texas. Suddenly there was a cracking voice from the wall speaker in Rex's room, and it said, "All campers of Amazonia, we have got the breakfast done! Come up and have it when it's hot! Or else it would attract the howler monkeys and Agelaia fulvofasciatas!". "Well then, it's time for our dreams to come true! You really don't when it is good times' in the forest! Let's get moving!" and saying that, Rex sped off to the canteen. We followed him to the canteen. It was quite an old building, and it looked like even a sneeze could make the whole thing topple over. We came closer to the building and saw Rex standing near it, his palm placed over it. "My dad's quarters when he was with Billy, the owner of Amazonia. dad always wanted to make something out of this place. He wanted all the people of the world to enjoy nature. He foresaw the destruction of nature long before anyone could predict it," he said emotionally. To tell the truth, even I was touched to hear it. He suddenly stiffened up and entered the canteen, where everyone was having their fill. I quickly had my breakfast. Not so big. I was too excited to eat anything big. I just had some cornflakes and milk. Well, actually, I must have eaten some Sorbombs too. Mom joined us after a few minutes. I got bored. On top of that, the canteen wasn't the most comfortable place to be. The frying sound of bacon and eggs, the clanging of metal, and the feet of chefs zipping and zapping throughout the place with the smaller children crying in shrill voices for chocolate—it was just mayhem in there. I couldn't stand the heat of the kitchen after some time. I think there isn't even a chimney in there, and soon I was sweating like a water sprinkler. I was still wearing that jacket because I am seated near the open windows, and the cold air rushes into my skin. I couldn't tolerate it anymore. So, I plopped myself into the jacket and went for a stroll outside the canteen. Outside the canteen, I could still hear the sound of some children. Not crying, but playing. I followed the sound until I found a mini-survival park right behind the canteen. Many children were jumping about in the puddles. Some were flipping the rocks to find some insects or creepy crawlies. Only some of the children seemed to be from other countries. Most of them were native people who came there for their holidays. It was actually the period when schools in Brazil gave long holidays. So, we could definitely expect some crowds. One of the boys was attempting to clear the hanging bridge. It was just a small bridge with broken wooden tiles. It was tied to a steel rope covered by a tube, and it wobbled like crazy. We need to jump above them to complete it. He was extremely agile. Jumping about on the bridge, it almost seemed like he was very familiar with it. But I didn't care about him.

Who is that boy?

I turned around and headed towards the canteen. But something didn't seem right about that place. I always felt sparks climbing up my spine. I turned around and saw that all the boys had just vanished. all except the boy who was attempting to finish the hanging bridge. Suddenly, he stopped and just kept standing for a few seconds. Then I saw his neck slowly turning around. Then he saw me with a very, very unexplainable, villainous grin. The next thing I knew, he pounced on me and grabbed my mouth. For a second, I was shocked, and my hands were paralysed. He punched me in the face, and that is when I came to life. I tried to yell, but I couldn't because he clapped his hands in my mouth. But he made a huge blunder by not holding my legs because they were really flexible and long. He was perched upon my chest, so I gave him a whack on his back with my legs. He fell over my side, groaning about something in Brazilian or Spanish. But the bigger hit was for me because my legs weren't strong; they were skinny. So, I sprained my foot. I quickly got up and hopped on one leg, rushing to the canteen and shouting, "Help! Mom! dad! Somebody help!" But it was too late; the last cook, who seemed to be old, had left his earpiece hanging on his neck, and everyone else had finished their breakfast and had gone to the safari bus. I had to get there as quickly as possible, and that was why I was limbering my foot around like crazy. But that boy jumped up quite quickly, bellowed like a rhinoceros, and charged towards me. I am not like some fighters or bullies. I am the one who is bullied by others. He leaped into the sand and grabbed my leg, and I tripped. I fell onto the sand, and that's when I got an idea. I quickly grabbed some sand, and when he pulled me up, I threw the sand into his eyes.

He was shouting something now and waving his hands like crazy! He couldn't open his hands and was rubbing his eyes. I thought of running, but I stopped. What use was it? He would catch me again anytime soon. I had to knock him down. I saw a small rock just beside me, and I grabbed it and gave him a nice whack on the head. At the same time, I made sure I didn't push the rock right into his skull because my idea was to immobilise him and not prepare a coffin. He fell down and stayed like that. A big bump was forming on his head. It was quite bruised. I quickly started running towards the safari camp management. I was dragging my feet because that guy had a really strong backbone, and that bent my foot. Luckily, I heard dad calling out "James! James! Where is that guy now?" I heard him, and I quickly shouted with all my might, "DAAAAAAAAAD!" and I fell on the heap of dry leaves right beside Rex's room. I heard Rex's voice, and I also heard the footsteps of my dad. I landed just there, on the heap of leaves, panting like a dog on a summer afternoon. dad spotted me and cried, "James! Where were you? Who did this to you?" Rex also joined the scene. "Who did this to you, boy? Who was it?" Rex said this in a state of distress. I pointed to the boy who had attacked me previously. The next thing I knew, I just closed my eyes. I didn't faint; I just felt tired after all the quarrels. After this incident, I would not even land my feet at the park, even if my life depended on it. I opened my eyes and found a whole new world in front of me. I was in Rex's room, and I could sense the smell of Rex. I rose up. I landed my legs on the floor. My leg is quite fine now. I walked on the floor for some time. Now, my leg was just perfect. The next thing I knew, the doors slammed open, and I saw that boy all tied up with his mouth plastered. I was so shocked by this sudden explosion that I jumped onto the bed. "We have caught him fair and square!" dad said it in a heroic voice. As for Rex, he was completely silent.

It was awkward because, during all the problems we had before, he used to be the first to get involved in them. This time, he was so quiet. He didn't even show his teeth. "Speak up, boy!" shouted dad into his mobile phone to translate it into Brazil's common language, Portuguese. dad ripped the plaster from the boy's mouth, and he screamed in a frenzy. I didn't even know a single word. In the translator, it showed these words: 'Someone told me to do this. "Who said it?" said dad in the translator, and there was another voice from the translator, and the boy replied something. The translator showed these words: 'I don't know his name. But I have seen him in my colony. He is known to be a smuggler. I gasped. This boy was in the hands of a smuggler. dad said, "Leaving this boy free would be dangerous. He would either be killed, or the smugglers may use this boy to know our whereabouts. Let's keep him like this. I followed dad and Rex out of the room. We followed the pavement and reached the safari bus. It was packed with people. All the seats were occupied. Mom was in there too. But it was all part of our plan. We switched seats with others. But we didn't change Mom's seat, so we kept her out of this whole search. "So, where do we sit?" I asked. "It is right there, in that corner." Rex said it in a cheerful manner. I thought it might be a pickup truck ready to tear up the tracks. But little did I know that I was in for an utter shock.

-

A disastrous truck goes into the forest!

I knew I was going to be shocked, but not in the worst way. It was a pickup truck. But I don't think it was insured because it was all rusted up. The windows were looking so weak. The tyres seemed to have some kind of crack. The hinges of the door were corroded. Overall, the car had a horrible image. It looked like someone recked while going for big air in the DRC. "What kind of thing is this?" my dad asked Rex, gasping for air. "It is the one and only Jeep J-10! The classic 1970 pickup! It is hot and heavy, ready for action! Bring on the heat!" Rex said it with a great deal of excitement. I did not see this before. I don't know his date of birth. But if his birth date was during the 1970s, then there is no mistake in loving a car like that.

To break my shock, the driver of the safari bus honked loudly, indicating that time was ticking. Rex went near the Jeep and called for us. I came walking, hesitating more and more with each step. At last, I kept my foot near the truck. It was in bad shape. I went for the door handle with trembling hands. I pulled up my guts at the last second and grabbed the handle. I think I grabbed it with too much power because there was a clang. I took my hand quickly from the handle, and the door rested just like that. It creaked slightly, and I didn't like the sound of that. Slowly, the top of the door faced down. But I didn't notice it. I only knew that the door was falling when the creaking became louder. I jumped backward in the nick of time to avoid the door. Rex didn't like to see that. "Easy there! It is a great Jeep! You're ruining it!" So much for a great Jeep. If the door ever fell down while driving amidst a pack of wolves, that's that. The end of me "How could I even get in?" dad screamed.

Don't you know how to enter the Jeep without the doors?" Rex asked, slightly fed up with the whole scene. "That doesn't make any sense!" dad shrieked. "Oh, you wait and see. Just watch and learn." Rex said with a huff of air and quickly slipped into the windows and landed in the driver's seat of the Jeep! It looked like he had some experience in car robbery; he looked like Tom Cruise on a highly confidential mission. I followed the same It was like a Nascar driver. I made it in without a scratch. But dad, his belly didn't make it in. "My belly is blocking me!" dad complained. Luckily, Rex struck a positive note this time. "That door works just fine; the only problem is that it's loose. So hold on to it tightly!" Rex warned dad. So, dad entered the Jeep, and Rex turned the key. There was a huge amount of rattling, and the Jeep turned on, rattling like crazy. My whole body was vibrating. It felt like my bone was trying to push its way through my muscles. When Rex pressed down on the accelerator, the car jetted out of the back gate of The Amazonia resort. The road was actually metal, and it was very smooth to ride on it. The safari bus was way ahead of us. Soon, we reached the first section of the safari, the Tapir Forest. The gate was actually different. There were two gates. The first one was facing us. Two guards with rifles opened the gate, and we entered the empty space in the middle of the gate. I saw behind me, and the gate was closed. It was an innovative way of separating the forests from other animals. The two guards who opened the first gate appeared again and opened the second gate, and it was completely a new world after that. There was a dense forest on the other side of the gate. The Jeep revved into the forest, and the gate closed behind us. It was very humid in the forest. After travelling some distance, we saw small animals walking in the distance. "They are Tapirs! Look at their nose! They are dangling like a rope!" Rex laughed. The

Tapirs weren't afraid of the car. It was like they were waiting for this. "Why aren't the Tapirs afraid of us?" I asked Rex. "They are used to this! They have been here for years!" Rex said. We need to leave the Jeep at the third section and walk into the forest just like that!" Rex said. "What are the animals in the third section?" dad asked Rex. "They are sloth bears! They aren't dangerous, though. They are so slow that moss grows on their backs. But the map shows that we need to go from the third section to the dangerous fourth section. That means we need to cross the Jaguar nest." Rex said. "Wh-wh-what do you mean about the Jaguar nest? Is it dangerous?" I stammered, feeling terrified. "Apparently, they are tamed Jaguars." Rex started. I huffed a sigh of relief. "And they are also adapted to the surroundings. They behave quite friendly to the meat feeders." Rex spoke slowly after a short gap. I was so relieved after that. "But the bad news is, they don't like me because I was the one who saved them from the forest fire." Rex said it again. "Why should they hate you? You saved their lives." dad asked. "They think that I separated them from their habitat. So, they will be very angry with me. In fact, this scratch on my hand is because of one of the Jaguars; he is the leader, Steven. If we could just speed through, we could escape." Rex said. He was trembling. He curled up his sleeve to show the scratch. It was a very long claw mark along his arm. But when I saw it suddenly, it looked like it was a tattoo, but then it looked like a scratch. I'm doubting this whole "dramatic scene" now. Could it be? Could it be that Rex wasn't the real Rex after all? Was I overthinking it? Maybe he is Rex after all. The jeep went bumping through the forest. The road was clean, and the safari bus was right in front of us. There were Tapirs all over the place, and the scene was calm. Until the safari bus stopped, that is.

That was 'inspiring'

The travellers on the bus were trying to fit their heads out of the window to see the scene. Even Mom was interested in the scene, so I also paid attention to it. Everyone was seeing a tapir near the water. It was getting ready for a feast of plants in the water. When it stepped a hoof into the water, a humungous crocodile dived for it and snapped it shut in just a second. The squealing of the tapir was terrible, and the crocodile just waded back into the water. Rex said, "That is very inspiring. Look at the bravery of the crocodile. He is trying to kill all the tapirs here. So, we give him only one per three weeks. For the rest of the three weeks, the tapirs have only one water source, the pond in the middle of the enclosure with some of their most favourite plants." said Rex. I don't know what's so 'inspiring' about this. It makes me wonder what will happen in the forest. But I did have many doubts. "How are the Tapirs directed to the pond in the middle?" I asked out of extreme curiosity. "I think if you watch closely, you will spot some gaps near the pond." Rex said. I did see them. It was a small gap, like a place for a sliding gate. "The gaps are where the gates hide. Look! They are rising from the ground!" Rex exclaimed, and indeed, the gates were rising. There was a really sharp sound, and all the Tapirs took off to the other side of the road, hitting and fighting with each other. That was a nice innovation. The safari bus went on, and we followed them, and at the distant end of the road, I was able to see the gate to the next enclosure, the bird park.

The innovative bird hub!

It was just like before. There were two gates separating the enclosures. The gates were higher than the previous ones. Nevertheless, the birds will keep flying over the gates. So, why should they separate the enclosures? The birds can easily escape. But little did I know that it was marvellous on the other side. We went inside the first gate. The two guards quickly closed them behind us. Then the other gate was opened, and the sight was just so epic. It was a huge, and I mean HUGE, spherical-shaped dome made of glass. " This is the magnificent glass bird enclosure. Not to brag, but it is the biggest glass-made object and animal enclosure in the world. Thanks to dad, I forgot all about Christmas. I didn't even have the faintest idea of what was happening back at home. I was just so interested in this dome. All that I know is that dad must have spent a fortune to book this trip. I made a personal note to thank dad for the trip. Rex said in an exciting manner, "This thing is visible from space! View it on Google Earth if you like! Oh, wait, I forgot. You shouldn't turn on your mobile phones in this area. So, switch it off." Then he pressed the pedal, and the Jeep went rattling into the dome. "This is the second sector! The next sector is just minutes from us! So, be prepared!" Rex said. After entering the door. Rex jumped out of the Jeep through the window like a pro. "Come on! Get out! This is an interactive place, and the only interactive place in this whole safari!" Rex said. This was way more than I could handle. I quickly jumped out but stumbled upon my legs and fell. dad was so lucky because he could just touch the door and it would open up just like a Rolls-Royce. I got up and saw two sections of the dome. The parrot section and the harpy eagle section The way the dome was built was just unbelievable.

It looked like a real forest environment. The humidity was maintained consistently. My eyes went to the harpy eagles. They were just hard to spot in those trees. But when I saw a complete eagle, I almost fainted. It was as big as me. Suddenly, there was a huge deal of commotion among the group from the safari bus. I gathered with them and spotted Mom. "What are you looking at, Mom?" I asked. She just stretched her palm, which was full of sunflower seeds, and screamed "Martin!". At first, I didn't know what she was doing. But after some seconds, there was a toucan with a bright beak who perched upon Mom's hand. The next second All the people behind us started shouting different names in different English accents. The dome was filled with sounds like "Olivia!" "Kennedy!" "Ian!" and different birds landed on their hands, looking at them. They had a snack of sunflower seeds, and they were even sitting on their heads saying, and I literally mean saying, "Thank you!" and they flew away! After this whole shouting of names, everyone ran towards the place where the parrots were separated from the Harpy eagles. The tourist guide, who happened to be the driver of the safari bus, said, "We are going to feed the Harpy eagles with dears!" After saying this, the birdkeeper of the dome pushed an old-looking deer into the dome and ran away. The squeaking sound of the Harpy eagles was sharp and ear-piercing. My eardrums went flat after hearing the sound. Suddenly, a large eagle, larger than the other eagle I saw, swooped down with a loud squeak and caught the deer by its hooves. The deer grunted and bleated in a high-pitched voice, and the eagle just lifted it effortlessly from the ground. I was lucky that I was on the other side, because if I had been there in place of the deer, I would have been finished by those Eagles. After some watching of those magnificently coloured parrots, we took off to the next spot, the Sloth bears.

The sloth bears

The Jeep was rattling into the forest, and it was hotter than ever. I was supposed to hit others with snowballs. But I am being hit by the heat of the flaming sun. I was drenched from head to toe. So was dad. Luckily, I had some sunscreen with me. I quickly applied them. My skin was the most sensitive, so I bought some SPF 30 sunscreen. They lasted longer than SPF 15. dad didn't even care about his skin because he was already too old to care about that. He asked for some sunscreen for his bald head, as it was turning red. The gate was much smaller this time. For comparison, the gate for the Tapirs must be around three to four times higher than this Jeep. This gate was no more than 10 feet tall. Anyway, it must take ages for sloths to climb the gate. We entered the gate and went into the dense forest again. This time, I could just see trees. "Where are the Sloths?" I asked. "They are just in these trees. You can't see them because they have moss on their backs. They are so slow, so it isn't difficult for moss to grow on them. It's great camouflage, though. So, they are difficult to spot." Rex explained. So, this place was basically a wasteland. You can't even see a soul in there. But my thoughts were wrong. I spotted a sloth slowly crawling near the road. It was just like watching a slow motion picture. It looked disgusting. Its back was green with moss. It had snot drooping from its nose. Overall, this thing was a disaster. Anyway, we followed the truck for some more minutes. Soon, we reached a place where the road split in two. The safari bus went right, while Rex turned sharply to the left. The safari bus soon went downhill and went out of sight into the forest while we were going down a different path, which was way darker. The road was really old and filled with portholes. Rex said,

"Alright, from here, we will stop at the fence and walk for about 5 miles. We would reach the spot in two hours without stopping while walking." "Wait, you said we would drive past the Jaguars." I said I was feeling a bit terrified. Rex replied quickly. "Oh, I thought of driving through the fence. But if I did so, the fence would be open, inviting the Jaguars for a feast. So, you know the consequences after that." dad piped in, saying, "Don't say we are going to walk through the Jaguar's enclosure. We would be doomed if we did." Rex said, "I am afraid that the answer is yes. Luckily, if you think on the bright side, we have our crossbows and tranquillizers. So, it isn't going to be a big deal." I had the feeling of going paranoid. The jeep was bumping into the portholes, and I felt my spine hurting a lot. This Jeep had such bad suspension. We soon reached the fence. It was a really old electrical fence, and half of the fence was rusted. "Well, here we are. If we just jumped over this fence, we would enter the Jaguar's enclosure. The crossbows are below the seat. I would have the tranquillizer, and you guys have the crossbows." Rex explained and jumped out of the Jeep. I slowly took the crossbow beneath my seat. I just tried to get it. The weight of the thing was more than enough to topple me down. I dragged it out of the seat, and with all my might, I lifted the crossbow and managed to throw it out. I jumped out after that and lifted the crossbow with both of my hands. I wore the strap around my neck. I hope the Jaguars don't catch a glimpse of me. I have seen many movies where people use crossbows. I knew how it functioned, so it was easy for me to use it. dad just came out, showing no attention to the crossbow. Rex said, "Alright, I hope you guys are ready. Shall we move?" he asked. I saw dad; he saw me back, and we both nodded to Rex's question. The moment had arrived. We were ready for an adventure!

The jaguar saw us!

Rex went ahead slowly. He saw us, then turned towards the fence. He slowly lifted his legs, getting ready to jump in, and suddenly, unexpectedly, a Jaguar came flying from the sky and roared right at Rex's face. To be honest, Rex wasn't even hazed by it. He just pressed his trigger, and it shot the Jaguar in the leg. It was just a matter of seconds, and the Jaguar was sound asleep. I, on the other hand, felt a sudden wave of goosebumps form all over my body and jumped with shock, even after handling the heavy crossbow, screaming at the top of my lungs. My dad was also so shocked by this sudden ambush that he caught hold of his crossbow and made a small jerk. I knew that he had a jerk because his belly was vibrating like crazy. Rex jumped over the fence and landed on the Jaguar, which was, you know, sleeping temporarily. I was kind of terrified because it is not every day you see a jaguar fall from the sky. "He was sleeping on the tree. Now we should keep moving, or else he would wake up!" Rex said it as if he could read my mind. I jumped over the fence quite easily. Not to brag or anything, but I actually got third place in the interschool hurdle race competition. So, I am pretty good at jumping. dad, though, couldn't even lift a leg. He couldn't jump more than a few inches higher than his height. But dad had other ideas in mind. There was a rock near the wooden pole to which the fence was tied. I knew what dad was thinking at the moment. He was trying to use the rock to climb the wooden pole and enter from the other side. He first stepped on the rock. It was a really flat and big rock that looked like it was built for a breakthrough. Then, dad lifted his other leg and landed it on the wooden pole. But things didn't go as planned. First, the wooden pole sank into the watery soil. Then, dad lifted his other leg and jumped to the other side. He landed straight on the jaguar's tail. You may think, What's so pathetic about it? But believe it or not, the jaguar had such a sensitive tail that it woke up. It groaned slightly, but that didn't stop it from seeing us. This time, Rex just took off. That sent us all into a frenzy, and we started running, and the jaguar started charging at us. It was really fast. Rex started climbing a tree. dad also started climbing a tree. This one was really old. Then what about me? Well, I was stuck on the ground, thinking of what to do next. Rex was searching for his darts. dad didn't know how to load the crossbow. I was standing on the ground with the jaguar standing face-to-face in front of me. My legs were paralysed. I was stuck to the ground. My hands were shaking instantly, and I was unable to move them. My mind went blank. The jaguar circled around me. I came to life when the jaguar snarled at me. Suddenly, a stone came flying from the air and smacked the head of the jaguar, and it roared like a rocket taking off. This roar was like a sonic boom. I lost my footing and fell to the ground. My eardrums went static. It was dad who threw the stone, and the jaguar went after him. The one skill that dad has is climbing trees like a pro. The jaguar climbed the tree, and dad quickly went running on a thick branch. But count the jaguar in the game because it is a born climber. It quickly approached dad and started ambushing him on the tree. dad slowly retreated. The jaguar kept walking closely towards dad. His teeth were the scariest thing to look at. dad was at the end of the branch, and the jaguar had just found its opportunity. It pounced on dad! I shouted like crazy. But what happened there? dad just jumped from the branch, and the jaguar slid on the branch and was hanging on the end. dad got hold of a long vine hanging from the tree. The jaguar tried to climb the branch for dear life. It tried to jump onto the branch. But in that process, it lost grip and fell down. dad slowly descended from the vine like a hero. But the more important thing was that the jaguar survived. dad started boasting in a majestic voice, saying, "Try to learn from me! This is called perfect tactics! Could you do that, James?". I was huffing. You know, dad boasts a lot. dad kept on boasting. But when I saw what was behind him, I just froze. It was the same jaguar snarling at him. His boastful talk had made him deaf. "dad! Behind you!" I shouted, but in vain. The next second, it pounced, and that's when dad just saw behind it. dad was so surprised by it. I was able to see the fear in his eyes. I closed my eyes. All I did was listen. I heard a sound like something flying through the air, and there was a thud. I opened my eyes and saw something completely unbelievable.

What just happened?

The jaguar was lying down with its eyes closed. It had all four of its legs spread out. It looked like a carpet. Suddenly, the leopard moved slowly, and from beneath it, dad came out with a very frozen face! "This place..." dad started, trembling with fear, "This is completely cursed! It has a death wish written all over it!" said dad. I saw the same kind of syringe that Rex shot at the Jaguar near the fence. So, it is pretty obvious now. It was Rex who had shot the jaguar! "Why did you take so long to shoot it?" I asked. It felt a bit suspicious. That guy was chilling on the tree for all this time. He is an expert forest survivor. Why didn't he shoot the Jaguar before? Rex replied, "I think I lost the darts!" I was about to break down right there. "But luckily, I found them hanging on the higher branches of the tree!" I huffed a sigh of relief. dad laid still. Rex climbed down the tree and said, "We don't want to waste time. Quick! Let's move before the leopard is awake!". dad got up, and we continued into the forest. Rex had the map. He kept looking into it and surveyed the environment. I was following him. The heat was unbearable. There were a lot of trees around us, forming a canopy. Even after being in the shade, the heat was getting intense. The soil beneath us was very loose and wet. My legs kept sinking under the mud. I luckily wore my boots instead of my slippers. Therefore, I didn't worry about the mud. But I always had the awful feeling that someone (or something, GULP!) was spying on us. Rex suddenly stopped dead in his tracks and indicated that we should remain silent. The moment we remained silent, there was a pleasant sound coming straight ahead of us. Suddenly, Rex burst out into a frenzy and said, "We have reached the waterfall!" and he quickly took off. I have to say, I was pretty impressed by how Rex located the waterfall on the map. I was also excited because I was dying of thirst and my canteen was empty. dad, who was huffing and puffing all the time, suddenly had a smile on his face and a burst of energy. He quickly ran after Rex. I, too, was running after him. The sound was getting more and more intense. The sound of rushing water The air was suddenly getting cooler. That's when Rex made a pit stop again. This time, he hid in a bush. We followed him in there. "The waterfall is the first milestone. We have achieved it!" Rex said. I was happy to hear it. "But... There is a problem," Rex said again. This time, my face drooped. I have already had enough trouble for a day. "The place of the waterfall is the place where the Jaguars' enclosure is present. So, we need to have a quick getaway. Keep your bottles open. We would need water. Because after this waterfall, there is no source of water for over 2 miles." Rex said. He didn't have to warn me, though; I had both my canteens and water bottles ready for filling. "Whatever you do..." started Rex again. "Don't STEP INTO THE WATER!" he said in a spooky voice. Then he opened his canteen, and dad took out his water bottle. Rex started counting down from three. When he barely said jumped up and ran as fast as lightning. We followed him, and he quickly filled his bottle. dad did the same. I had two canteens and a water bottle, so it took me some time to fill the bottles. I filled the two canteens simultaneously. The opening of the bottle was too small, and it was hard for the air to pass out. Suddenly, I heard a growl, and I didn't need to hear that twice because I knew exactly who it was.

The Jaguar is hungry!

I quickly closed my canteens, and I got hold of my water bottle and started filling it like crazy. A new Jaguar entered the scene, and it was growling at me. I desperately needed water because there is no water source for the next 2 miles. So I had to hurry up the process. The bottle was completely filled, and the jaguar was getting closer and closer. "Come fast, James! Leave the bottle!" shouted dad. I was able to see a greedy grin in its eyes. I partially closed the bottle and took off. The jaguar wasted no time and started chasing me. I ran and ran, but I was no match for the jaguar. The jaguar was just beside me. I screamed with fear. But there was nothing I could do. The jaguar grabbed my arm with its paws, and two of its claws pierced my shoulder. It felt like some acid had been poured down my shoulder. I shouted and squealed like a pig. Soon, there was a familiar sound, and I quickly got to know what it was. There was a thwack, and the jaguar fell down. I quickly grabbed my canteen, which fell down, and I ran towards Rex and dad. Blood was flowing from my arms, and there was nothing I could do about it. I saw dad, and he quickly ran towards the waterfall and ran to the pond. Rex shouted, "Don't go near it!" but dad turned a deaf ear. He started filling his other bottle with water and came running towards me. He poured all of the contents on my arms, and I felt satisfied. The water from the pond is really cold because of the waterfall churning it up. Rex was actually feeling terrified! He said, "I told you not to go near the pond. You have disturbed Makra!". dad said, "What a strange name? Who is this?" But before he could complete his sentence, there was a loud splash. Under the glare of the sun, I thought it was a log flying in the sky. But when it landed, I turned pale.

Well... Who do we have here?

There was a huge crocodile in front of us. When I say humungous, I literally mean it. That ancient thing must have been 20 feet tall, and it was growling. "Why did you disturb that estuary?" He is the biggest crocodile in the whole of the Amazon!" Rex shouted. It didn't take much time for the Croc to start chasing us. Rex took off, as did me and dad. Suddenly, Rex started running in zigzags, and he said, "Run like me!" I knew why he told me that, and I kind of felt sorry for myself for not knowing it beforehand. The crocodile is a fast runner; I accept that. But it is a fast runner only in a straight line because it is CRAWLING! It can't change lanes suddenly. dad was also following me, and we ended up escaping from that croc. Rex said, "I am so surprised; I didn't see more than two jaguars in this enclosure. I think it is our luck." Rex said. "Why?" I asked back, panting. "Because we have reached the end of the jaguar enclosure!" Rex said it in a majestic voice.

Steve has arrived

I was really happy that I had achieved a milestone. It was a proud moment for me. dad was also happy to hear it. He was sweating from head to toe and had a really bad smell. Rex said, "Now, we follow the same procedure. We will jump over this fence and run away as fast as..." But before he could finish, there was a roar coming from the forest. "It's time to leave this place," said Rex, and he took off. I followed him along with dad. We jumped above the fence, and we were running again! The roar was getting a bit louder now, and Rex was running like mad, shouting, "Help! Aaaaaahhhhh!". The roar was getting more intense by the minute. There was a rustling of leaves from above. I took one peek above me, and I saw a shadowed figure jumping about in the trees. I knew what it was. It overtook Rex and landed right in front of him, snarling. It was a Jaguar, and it was eyeing Rex like it was its only meal for a year. "Well, hi Steve! Good day, isn't it?" Rex said. The jaguar pounced on him. Rex quickly took a mouthguard from his pocket and shoved it into the jaguar's mouth. Anyway, the spikes in his belt and shoes had already pierced the jaguar, and it was wailing. I quickly ran and jumped over the fence. Rex was shouting and waving his hands like crazy. I quickly lifted my crossbow and tried to aim the jaguar. But it was really hard. I waited for the perfect time and pressed my trigger, and the dart went flying in the air. I watched as it flew and pierced something. I blinked my eyes, and for a moment, things were dark. As soon as I opened my eyes, I saw the dart had hit Rex's finger, and he wasn't moving. There was another swish in the air, and the Jaguar lay flat on the ground. dad went near the Jaguar cautiously and pulled Rex with all his might. Rex didn't make a move. His heart was still beating, but he was tranquillized. dad quickly slapped him, and he woke up, startled by all the drama. He quickly got up and stumbled on his legs. He mumbled, "Run," and he stumbled above the fence. dad followed along, and we ran after we reached a safe distance. We had successfully covered half of the path. But there was still more to this adventure.

The next 2 miles

First and foremost, I was exhausted as a result of everything that had occurred. So, I seriously needed some rest because even the weather wasn't helping me. Second, I wanted food because I was really, REALLY hungry. Now that I think of it, I had breakfast about four hours before. I took a look at my watch and almost fainted. It was 3:00 o'clock in the afternoon! The heat was frying me. All I could do was feel sorry for myself. The condition of dad was worse. He was wearing his favourite black full-hand shirt and his jeans, and the temperature was much, much worse. With all these inappropriate dresses, dad was turning red with heat. The black shirt did no good. I just didn't see him because, looking at his condition, I started sweating immediately. Only Rex was in tip-top shape, and he started watching the map.

I had completed one of my canteens almost instantly. "I would pay anything to go back to that waterfall. I don't mind that alligator." I said. "It was a crocodile, not an alligator." Rex said. "Whatever it is! I was just saying it. I didn't mean it!" I exclaimed, Frustrated." I took my other canteen, and I poured the whole of it on my head. I was steaming. dad couldn't take it anymore. He leaped for his bag and poured the water into his shirts, and I swear that I heard a hissing noise from somewhere. Rex said, "Quick, we need to get moving before night. I didn't know why. As if he read my mind, he quickly told me that it was a nasty place to be at night. Especially at 12:00, when tarantulas come out to eat the dead. That information was enough for me. I didn't want my head to be buried by a spider. So, I stood on my feet and started following Rex. dad completely denied the idea of walking again because, to tell the truth, he was already a wreck by now. Rex was quick to answer. He said that by now, the treasure might decompose because it was really old. Every second counts. When dad heard that this run was related to money, he responded with a jerk and said, "What are we waiting for? Let's get moving!" Well, I said it before, and I am saying it now: these days, people are behind this thing called a bill. We were walking like nothing had happened. I had a bright smile. We had successfully escaped the jaguar's enclosure. We also completed 3 miles in record time. "Where are we?" I asked. "In the anaconda enclosure!" Rex spoke calmly. I gulped and turned pale. My smile faded away in a second, and my thoughts froze. "How long do we need to walk for the treasure?" my dad asked, petrified. "There is still a mile to complete. I don't know why you are trembling. Anacondas don't attack humans. That is, until we disturb them," said Rex without any sound of disturbance in his voice. The sun was now in the western hemisphere, and it could set anytime soon. If only we were quick enough.

I had completed the last bottle of water, and somehow it made me feel thirstier. I had also skipped lunch, and it wasn't helping me either. For dad, well, his stomach was grumbling once every minute. I couldn't bear it anymore and asked Rex, "I am hungry. Is there anything to eat?" Rex was quick to answer. "Why didn't you say so?" he exclaimed. "If you were hungry, I could have cooked you some leaves. It is all around us." Now that I think of it, I saw trees around me. Believe it or not, but I completely forgot we were in a forest—and not just any forest—the great Amazon Forest! Now, another thought stuck in my mind. We were in such a large forest, and we had been running frantically for 3 miles, I believe, and I don't know if I remember the way. How were we going to make it out of this place? Another gong hit my head! Now that the sun was setting, if Mom returned to the resort and found out that we hadn't arrived, she may complain to the resort, and if they found us in the forest, everyone would know about the treasure. Then, one thought led me to the other, and I was really scared. I asked Rex about all these problems, and he didn't seem too pathetic about them and kept on walking. We didn't have anything to eat. I didn't want to eat the leaves of trees, but dad was all in for it. He was basically like a cow that eats trees. In fact, dad was so hungry that he almost ate a mushroom without knowing it was poisonous. Luckily, I stopped him in the nick of time. He was just like a huge Pac-Man. It was already 5:00 in the evening, and Rex had some good news. He said that there was a clearing in our way and that we could sleep there. I asked if there would be any tarantula invasions, but he completely denied it. I also asked what we would sleep on, and he quickly shook his head, saying not to worry because he had a surprise that would blow my mind. I didn't know what 'surprise' he was talking about because, obviously, it couldn't be a surprise. I could hear the birds flying away into the trees.

Seeing the ground, another thought struck me. Rex said we were in the anaconda enclosure, and till now, I hadn't seen any anacondas. What was all the fuss about? Rex suddenly stopped and gestured for us to stop too. Then he took the map and carefully observed it. The chirping of the crickets was giving me the most obnoxious feeling, and it wasn't so great all right. "Here it is!" Rex exclaimed, finally breaking the silence. He took his sword and sliced away the bushes, which revealed the most amazing view—we had arrived at the clearing! When we ran to the clearing, to the far right, I was able to see the water rushing from a cliff and falling to the ground. "The treasure is just over the cliff!" Rex exclaimed. The view was extraordinary. The sun was setting behind the cliff, and the sky was turning red. The temperature was good enough, and the sound of the waterfall was also helping my mind relax. "What is the surprising thing you were talking about?" asked dad, who wasn't interested in the scenery. "Oh. Well, if you want it to be fast, I could show you right now. It's your wish," said Rex. "Do it now!" dad replied sluggishly. "Well then, here goes..." moaned Rex, and he quickly reached out for his backpack. He reached for the zipper, and when he opened the backpack, it was like a sudden explosion of something green. Add three iron rods along with that. It lay there on the floor, like a huge amount of slime spilled on the floor. Rex exclaimed with some delay, "It is a sleeping tent!" Well, the first impression wasn't so good. But Rex started working on the tent quickly. He started hammering the nails. Then he started tying the rope. Actually, I know how to tie a tent because I have been on a lot of school ranger trips and have learned to tie a tent as well. But now I was too tired to host a tent. So, I just sat down and watched Rex do all the work. In a few minutes, Rex had finished the job, and there was a massive tent right before me. I entered it inside, and it was warm and cosy. It had three sleeping bags, and in the corner of the tent, there was a pile of neatly tied firewood. It was a nice place to stay. "I also bought some edible plants on the way," said Rex. The tent was just great. I went out to call dad, but he was not present outside. I went inside to call Rex, who was pouring something into a glass. It was white, and it was definitely something fishy. He threw the bottle after pouring the contents into the glass and started cackling like a maniac! Something was fishy. Rex was acting weird. I quickly took the bottle and read it. It said fludrocortisone acetate. Caution: an overdose may make you faint for 29 hours!' I knew that Rex was brewing something. He was trying to faint. But other than dad and me, no one was in the forest. So, I made it clear that Rex was trying to make me faint. Now I knew what he was up to. Maybe he is not the real Rex or something. I thought of running away when a cold hand landed on my shoulders. "James, would you like some juice?" said Rex, who was not the real Rex. Now that I think of it, I knew he was not Rex. On the flight, The Rex that I saw didn't have any claw marks. How did Rex get them? I gulped. He was definitely a killer, and he is trying to loot the treasure! "N-no, I am go-good." I said I was trembling. "So, you found out my profession..." mumbled Rex in such a way that I started getting goosebumps on my back. I started to panic. He was about to get hold of me, but I slipped out of his hand, grabbed some sand, and threw it in his eyes. He moaned in anger, shouting, "Come here, filthy pest! Get him!" I made a run for my money and soon ended up at the same spot where we entered the cliff. If I go into the jungle, then I am done. I am not exactly the kind of guy who uses the stars to find his way out of a huge forest. So, I just swung around and thought of running the other way. But a huge man with a bald head came in my way. He had tattoos all over his body, even on his head.

He was the kind of guy you don't want to mess with. He snarled at me like a massive bull getting ready to charge. I quickly started running back, but it was too late because he had already lifted me up. I was wriggling and kicking him to let him go. But he wouldn't budge. I just thought of stopping because there was no way a 99-pound boy like me was going to defeat a 198-pound monster like that guy. Anyway, he was lifting me up with only one hand grabbing my leg. So, he is practically a Frankenstein of a guy. Suddenly, I noticed that there were seven more guys surrounding me, and one of them was very familiar. Wait a minute. It was the same boy who attacked me. He was laughing at me, as were the six other nitwits. So, who was Rex? Well, he wasn't present at the moment. He was in the tent. When he came out, he was no longer in the Rex costume. His face was like Rex's, but he was wearing a white suit. Just then I recognised who it was...

The reveal of the imposter

It was an international criminal smuggling rare redwood from the Amazon to Africa; it was Smith! And not just any Smith; it was Preston Von Smith! I recognised him because I had seen his dirty face in the NEWS. "Well, James. You may be surprised by this new outfit, and maybe you already know who I am. I am the twin brother of the famous Thomas Rex!" Now it made sense. "Where is my dad?" I asked Smith with irritation. "Ohhhh... I completely forgot. I think your dad wanted some 'juice'. So, I sent him into the forest to drink some!" sneered Smith. Now I was fuming! But suddenly, there was a Tarzan yell from behind us. I couldn't see what was happening, but everyone was running frantically. The big guy dropped me and started running as well. I turned around to see what the commotion was all about, and the sight made me tremble. There were a thousand short, brown guys yelling and playing drums. Many of them had blowpipes. Before I could run away, a dart pierced my fingers. Suddenly, I was feeling dizzy. I felt like taking a short nap, and then everything blacked out.

Intelligent civilizations or foolish cannibals?

When I woke up, I saw myself in the dense forest. The sound of the waterfall was still there, and it was actually morning. I felt something funny on my back. I kept a hand out, and suddenly there was a wiggling feeling. I quickly got hold of the thing and dropped it, shouting. It was a hairy, black, and red tarantula, and it was going nuts because I had just broken one of its legs! I screeched and yelled for help. But I was just paralysed on the spot. I couldn't move, and my mind froze. I had already had one encounter with a tarantula way back in the hotel room and didn't want to end up messing with it again. I was the butcher for the goats and the lord of the creepy crawlies. The tarantula was right at my feet, which were trembling with fear.

Suddenly, a large bush beside me began to twitch. I wasn't sure what it was, but I definitely didn't want to mess with it. I closed my eyes, hoping for the best. There was a familiar kind of 'swish that went past my head. I opened my eyes just to have a peek at what was going on, just to find the same small man with his blowpipe trying to make me faint again. Luckily, at that moment, I stopped feeling frightened and thought practically. I took off on my feet and made a run for it. But, strangely enough, the man didn't follow me. Instead, he was battling with the tarantula, which he was finally able to kill. It was squished to death then and there. Then the man took a wooden bowl and put the spider in it. He shot me a look that made my spine shiver. Then he spoke his first words to me in a deep voice, saying, "Follow me. Your *pepo* is waiting." His accent was really funny. It was like a French person trying to talk English. Whatever *Pepo* meant, it was like something was found. What was I missing? I followed the small man. He was quick and swift. On the way, he indicated that I stop and sniff the air. Suddenly, he jumped on one of the trees and started climbing it to the top. Obviously, I didn't know how to climb the tree, but I was terrified. Suddenly, there was a chirping noise, and I could see hundreds of birds flying away from the spot. What if it was an Ocelot? As more thoughts struck me, the man made his descent. He was holding a huge spider in his hands. It made me shriek at the top of my lungs. I was Arachnophobic, and I had enough of spiders already. "Stop shouting! It is crispy. Want to try-a?" Now I was feeling nauseous. I held my palms to my mouth and frantically shook my head. "You missed the treat. If you don't want it, I will eat it!" Saying this, the short man ate the spider. The crunch of the spider was enough for me. I went to the nearest bush and puked. The man shrugged and started running again. I didn't want to be stranded in the jungle. But I also didn't want to be eaten. That man may be a cannibal. Who knows? But I still followed him. There may be some intelligent civilization in the forest, and I could use that to get out. I could hear some faint sound from somewhere, and we were going towards it. The sound grew louder and louder. "Behold... the magic of the *fife*!" said the man, and he moved the bushes in front of us, and there was literally a whole colony in there with flames blasting out from unexpected places. I wonder why I couldn't view this area on Google Earth because the smoke was just taking off into the open sky. And did I mention that there were no trees in this place? Well, there were no trees except for one large, large tree in the centre of the ground. I wonder what it was for. The place was just great. The problem was that these people were more like cannibals. Yet they wore trousers and t-shirts like they were on vacation! It didn't make sense, but these people didn't seem too local. Those people looked like they were from the city. Suddenly, someone was smacking a drum with what looked like a bone. Soon, more drums followed, and the small pebbles below me started vibrating. A small guy from the top of the tree said, "Allow me to present the great king, Jingle Jonga!" Suddenly, there were the sounds of trumpets arising from the trees. It felt like some great king was about to be presented in front of us. And yes, it was a king. He was fat and chubby. He was wearing a necklace made of something that looked like bones. I hope they aren't human bones, though. "Welcome to the great Amazonia! Thanks for coming for dinner!" said the king. Suddenly, I felt something touching my shoulder, and I saw a short man who was as tall as me and who was holding a blowpipe. A thought quickly struck me, and I snatched the blowpipe from him. "Catch him!" cried the king, and as I had thought, these people were cannibals! I was shivering now, and I managed to get the blowpipe to my mouth. I quickly aimed for the king, and I blew the pipe with all my might. The dart went flying into the air, and everyone paused to watch the scene. It went and hit the stomach of the king, and it just bounced away. I had blown the pipe the wrong way. Everyone had their hungry eyes on me now, and I didn't know what to do. I just waved my hands, and they were running after me again! They were rounding me up from all directions. I just closed my eyes and said my prayers, hoping for the best. Suddenly, there was a huge yell, and the crowd just went nuts. I opened my eyes, and the crowd seemed to be frantically searching for a place to run away. I didn't know what they were so afraid of, but it meant trouble. In the huge crowd, I got pushed, and I fell to the ground. One of the guys ran over my back, and I squealed like a pig in fire. Anyway, no one cared about me. My back was aching, and I tried to get up, but I couldn't even budge. Soon, everyone was gone. I didn't know where they had run away, but I could tell that they were afraid of something. Maybe they were Arachnophobic like me. No, they weren't.

The gang is back!

It was just a familiar voice that made me paralysed. It was none other than Smith and his gang. They were all surrounding me, snickering. "Well, James, you must end up like your dad, I suppose. Lost in the woods with no idea what to do next. Tell you what, you made a big blunder by following civilization in the forest. These guys are under my feet!" roared Smith. I was turning red. He left dad in the forest. Now, where in the world would he be? I was just doomed now. If there were any Google satellites to pass by, it would be great. But the chances were slim. The gang slowly surrounded me. The boy who attacked me at the resort had a smug smile. I was in the dark. It was night, and I was just stuck in the middle of the biggest forest in the world. What could be worse? All I needed was a miracle. Now, the gang was just near me with clubs and stuff. Suddenly, there was a huge, piercing roar, and from the bushes came a huge leopard. Now where did this guy come from? The leopard was now ambushing us. The bushes suddenly began to move yet again, and this time, there were no leopards; it was my dad! Run, James! Quick!" shrieked my dad. I quickly ducked under the hands of one of the guys and started running away from the leopard. "RUUUUUNNNNNNN!" cried the guys in the gang, and they scattered away shrieking. "You fools! Catch him! Quick! Idiots!" shouted Smith. Only the small boy took attention, and he quickly came for me. I was running away from the pack into the forest, and unexpectedly, the tribal guys jumped out from their hiding spots with their clubs. Behind me was the boy who was running for me. I quickly thought of something and made up a plan. I stopped, turned around, and shouted, "dad, help!" This may not seem like a plan, but at that moment, that was the only plan I had. dad was still carrying his crossbow, and he had shot one of the people in the gang. The moment he heard my cries, he quickly pointed the crossbow at the boy and shot it at him. He fell to the ground, unconscious. I've started running away from the tribes now. The leopard was now stalking Smith. But Smith had his own crossbow. So he shot it at the leopard, and it fell to the ground, unconscious. I just have to escape the tribes now. dad was coming for me, and we quickly made a run for the forest. But it wasn't too soon. Smith had grabbed hold of my leg, and I fell to the ground. He quickly took his crossbow and shot dad at his leg, and dad fell down. His crossbow slipped from his hands and fell to the ground with a thud. The crossbow was close. If I was just able to reach it with my fingers. Smith was too busy reloading the crossbow. "You have done enough destruction! Now I would clear you and your dad and get the treasure for myself. The only thing sticking out of the crossbow was the dart. I tried to reach for the dart. Meanwhile, Smith was loading his dart. I was able to reach for the dart, but it was on the sharp side. If I were to grab it, then it would prick my hand, and my hopes are done. There was a faint grunt from behind me, and I knew that it was the leopard. This time, I quickly had a plan. "Not the leopard again! I would kill this boy now!" shrieked Smith with anger, and he placed his crossbow right at my neck. I quickly grabbed the dart and took it out of my hands, and at that moment, the leopard pounced to grab Smith. At that exact moment, I pierced the leopard's paw, and it pushed away Smith, who cried with pain, and everything went black.

The tribes turn good

I woke up just to see the sun blazing right into my eye. I quickly woke up and rubbed my eyes. Everything looked mismatched, and nothing was straight. I looked around. I was on the same stretcher again, and this time there were no tarantulas. dad was right beside me with a huge cloth spinning in his hands. "Where is Smith?" I asked out of curiosity. "He is no more," replied dad in a hoarse kind of voice. "Did you know that he wasn't the real Rex?" I asked dad. This time, dad smiled and replied, "I indeed knew he was not the Rex from the Jeep." I was startled. "Why didn't you say so?" I asked with my mouth open in shock. "Didn't you find something funny with that tiger claw mark?" I revised my thoughts about the Jeep drive, and yes, it looked like it was a counterfeit. "Yes, I did notice it. From one angle, it looked like a tattoo to me." I said. "Exactly. I knew it was the twin brother of Rex. Read it in the newspaper during the flight. Now things became a bit clearer to me. "But how did you bring that Jaguar—I mean the leopard—with you?" I asked again. "I just waved some fire and started running. It was chasing me down, and I quickly threw some of Smith's torn coat to the ground and climbed the tree. I wasn't sure if it would follow the scent, but miraculously, it did." Now things became even more clear. "Did you ever wonder where we are?" asked dad. "How am I supposed to know? I don't have any." I stopped for a moment. "Wait... the map... the tent..." I was straining my mind. I definitely sensed something funny, and I don't want to miss it. "I know!" I exclaimed, jumping a foot and landing back on the ground. "I know! Smith had a GPS! I saw that in the bag at the Jeep drive. I kept my bag in the tent! There is a way out of this forest! We are saved!" I exclaimed, doing a small dance. "Do you mean... this?" said dad, taking out a small rectangular device that looked like a Lego NXT controller. It wasn't the controller, though; it was the GPS! "How did...*gasp*..." I lost my words. "Just from the bag!" said dad, winking. This was definitely a moment to celebrate. But the sound of the bushes faded my smile, and suddenly there was a small man from the same tribe, and he was looking through his bushy eyebrows at us. "The tribes..." I whispered to dad. "Don't worry, these guys are good!" exclaimed dad. "We are happy! Thank you for saving us!" said that small man. "Who did we save them from?" I asked dad. "Smith, of course!" he replies. Now things make sense. I took the GPS and saw that we were close to the Amazon River. If we could cross that river, then after half a mile, we could reach the Trans Amazon Highway! With luck, we could get some lift, and then we would be off from this dangerous, flea-bitten place. Oh, and I forgot to say that the New Year was yesterday. I hate this Christmas vacation so much. I don't know if there will be any presents. I told dad to pack up because I had found our spot. But dad said to wait. "We came here for the treasure, and we shouldn't leave it. These people are so attached to the treasure that they guard it day and night with their soldiers. We need to get that somehow, and I've already planned our heist.

The heist of our lives!

The man led us back to the tree, and the king, Jingle Jonga, was so happy. The other people bowed at our feet. They didn't know English. So he spoke something gibberish, and the small man translated it. "Ask us anything you want," said the man. Quickly, dad asked the whereabouts of the treasure. The small man turned rigid for a moment, then he said something to the king, and in turn, he frowned and replied something. The small man said, "King-a says no-a. He asks for anything else," he said. "Do you have a car?" asked dad. "Yes-a!" exclaimed the small man. "Show us that car." asked dad again, and the small man whispered something in the king's ear, and he started jumping and ran into the bushes. The king also went behind him, and we too ran behind him. He led us into an old go-down where farmers usually park their tractors, and in that go-down, there was a jeep. Not the Jeep that Smith was driving. This one was a Jeep, which looked completely new, and it was rather old. I think it is a Jeep CJ from the 1970s. The words *Cordrey M. Sullivan* were etched on the licence plate, which didn't have any numbers. "Give us the key. We want this Jeep," asked dad. The little man whispered something to the king, and he quickly removed the pendent that he wore and gave it to dad. He winked at me, and we went back to the tree. It was afternoon, and dad said his plan in a very isolated place. "I spotted the place where they guard the treasure. Me and you will go to that very spot. You try to distract them for a second. I will quickly take that treasure, and we will run away in the Jeep!" explained dad. The problem was that we still didn't know that the Jeep was filled with gasoline. So, we went down again and saw that there were two barrels of gasoline in the Jeep. We opened the gas tank cap and saw that it wasn't filled.

So, we luckily managed to avoid any hiccups during the heist. We thought of our path and found out that the path I speculated was right over the canyon. So we had to take the longer route. We need to go through the colony and straight into the forest, and then take a right to go down an inclined slope that the people over here built. Another problem was that the Amazon River was right in our way. Smith had a binocular, and we quickly took it and ran to the edge of the cliff, which wasn't so far. From there, we saw that most of the river was open except for one part where a bridge connected the two sides. From there, we could get away onto the Amazon highway, and then it is just straight to Lodgia Amazonia! Even if it did seem complicated, the heist is pretty simple. So, exactly at noon, we went to the spot, and as dad said, four soldiers stood at four corners, and right in plain sight was the treasure. I thought of throwing stones at them and then running away. But I didn't want to lose my skin. So, I just covered myself with bushes and slowly moved towards the guards. At first, the guards didn't seem to notice. But when I came a tad closer, they became alert. I quickly screamed and ran away. Three of them came chasing me, and one of them stayed there, guarding my chest. I quickly ran into the bushes, and the soldiers still followed me. One of them threw a spear, and it came flying above my head. I ran with all my might, and I felt the spear handle brushing my back. It missed the spear by an inch! I kept running, and a few more spears came flying by. But what terrified me more was that there was an ear-piercing shout that had a rhythm to it, and all the soldiers stopped and ran back. I quickly took off to go down and saw the Jeep right there. The problem was that I didn't have the keys, and the doors were locked. dad must have been coming behind, and he sure was. He entered the go-down and quickly placed the key into the keyhole of the door, and with a click, the doors unlocked. We quickly got in, and dad turned the keys to the Jeep. But it didn't start. dad tried frantically to start the Jeep, but it didn't. dad gave up the keys, and he opened the bonnet. We still didn't have time. From somewhere far away, we could hear some shouting. dad was doing something, and he quickly said, "James! Get me some motor oil!" and I got down to the shelf and saw that there was an old and dusty motor oil bottle. I passed it to dad, and he filled the engine with the oil. He didn't care to use a funnel. He filled it to the brim, and we went into the jeep. It was getting late. The voices were now getting louder. dad tried to rev the Jeep to life, and at last, with a huge rattle, the Jeep woke up. dad quickly pressed the accelerator, and we took off, leaving a lot of dust behind us. It seemed like the whole town was behind us. Suddenly, I asked, dad, where is the chest?" dad suddenly slammed the brakes. I quickly opened the door and ran to go down with the chest. By now, there were so many people behind me that I had to just throw the chest into my seat. dad took off without any notice, and I was hanging on to the Jeep by holding the seat and the door. I was hanging, and the people threw spears and rocks at me, and they barely missed the Jeep. I threw myself inside and closed the door, and we were blazing down into the town! There were just one or two tribes there. So, we had no problem escaping from civilization. But what made us feel so frightened was when a spear came flying right into the back window of the Jeep and shattered the whole window. The spear landed perfectly at the back seat, and the sharp edge barely missed the tank of gasoline behind it. We followed the GPS, and we came to the slope. It was fairly decent. It was still a bit steep, so dad had to carefully drive the Jeep. But the problem was that there was a terrifying hairpin just down the line, and it was getting narrow, and it didn't have any guard rails. If we ever fell down, it would be two trips. One is to the base of the mountain, and the second is to death! dad had to do this turn perfectly. He was going slower than ever, and the tribes were following behind. dad made the turn somehow and sped again down the slope. But the slope got narrower and narrower until the only option was to get down and run away. But we can't do that. dad managed to make the hairpin, and we were only a few feet from the ground. The next hairpin was impossible to go through, and if we were to fall, it would be in the river. dad suddenly shouted, "Put on your seatbelts," and hearing his roar, I quickly pulled the seatbelt from behind. Before I could even fit it into place, dad turned sharply to the left, and we were falling for a few seconds to the ground, tyres facing down. There was a sudden stop, and my skull seemed to have misaligned. The tribes were throwing spears. dad quickly took the wheel and raced down the side of the river. The bridge was getting closer and closer, and the tribes were falling back. We reached the bridge and drove the Jeep above it, and the probability of us escaping was high. That was until the pillar below the bridge broke. I thought that we were done. But dad was one good driver. He quickly shot out in 5th gear, and the tiles were falling behind us. It was like death chasing us down. dad made some air at the end of the bridge, and we were riding in the dense forest, the tribes frantically searching for a way to cross the river. It was about midday, and the sun was blazing. Here we are, riding happily, escaping the tribes to see life as we knew it. I couldn't wait to see Mom. She must have been so worried. We soon heard the sound of some trucks, and there we were! We had successfully reached the Trans-Amazonian Highway! I thought of crying. Two nasty days in the forest What could go wrong?

Back to Lodgia, Amazonia!

The smell of tar rose in the sky. Getting to sniff them is one of the most pleasant things to do after getting stuck for over two days in the wild. dad took out his GPS and revved the Jeep. It was a three-hour journey. On our way, we stopped at a grocery store and had some water and (at last) food! I hadn't drunk water for like 2 days, and I was hungry as well. We rode into the setting sun. I dozed off for a few minutes. I woke up when something tossed me up in the Jeep. We had reached the rugged path up to Lodgia Amazonia, and there were helicopters taking off from the spot. There were a lot of media trucks as well. Wondering what happened, we quickly went to Lodgia Amazonia, just to witness hundreds of people buzzing around the Jeep. We opened the door, and suddenly people were swarming around us. They were reporters, and they were sticking their microphones into our mouths and noses. The cops somehow cleared the crowd. "How are you, sir? Are you fine? Are you injured? You are to visit the police station and say everything you know," said one of the cops. We were flabbergasted. We went into our room. Mom was crying on the bed. When she saw me and dad, especially in muddy, torn clothes, she came running and hugged us. "Where have you been these two days? I was waiting for you. What went wrong? Where were you?" she said with worry and sorrow. "Everything for our good Mary. We just found a huge chest of treasure in the wild!" assured dad to Mom, who had now changed. "And why did you go to the forest without saying a farewell to me? How AM I SUPPOSED TO MAKE Christmas CARDS myself? Where COULD I GET A TEMPLATE? IN YOUR HEAD?" shrieked Mom in her usual, commanding voice. One second later, she was crying. The next moment, she changed her whole face. This was such a sudden change that even dad was flabbergasted. The media swarmed around us for two days, and I did my best to spice up the adventure. I included some tranquillizing robots that attacked us with their laser eyes. I know that you wouldn't believe me. But the reporters just needed a story to make their broadcast better, and they believed every word like a hypnotised guy serving for us. I didn't mention the civilization, though. They were the only ones in the forest, and they were native too. If these people heard about these guys, they would kill them. "We heard that Von Smith is on the run after bursting out of prison. What do you think about him?" asked one of the reporters, and my thoughts quickly sparked in my mind. "We met a forest ranger named Rex, who is supposed to be the twin of Von Smith. But then we found out that he was actually Von Smith in disguise. He was trying to grab the treasure. I grabbed my mouth. I had spilled the beans! The next second, everyone stuck up their noses like they had smelled something funny, and then everyone was sticking their microphone in our noses and asking about their treasure. We had no other option but to confess. "Yes, we found a treasure. But we found out that it was really old. So, we are handing it to the archaeologists who could do research about the treasure." I quickly said the first thing that struck my mind, and now dad was glaring at me angrily. The next moment, I changed the topic to Von Smith, and I quickly concluded that I didn't know if he was alive or dead. Somehow, the management shoved the mob out of the lodge. dad was now really angry. What could I do? "Why don't we take half of the money for ourselves?" I asked. dad suddenly shot a look. He then went to the chest and kept it on the bed. That's when I remembered that we had forgotten to see what was in the chest! The moment had arrived! dad saw me, and I saw dad. We mentally approved that we were ready. dad took a deep breath, and so did I. Then, without any notice, dad flung open the chest, and he jumped down to the floor, trembling. I gathered some courage and poked my head in the chest, only to be glared at by the amount of light reflected by the chest. There were heaps of gold! There were coins, jewels, ornaments, and more! There were many drawings etched on it. Our flight was for tomorrow, and we have a friend called Jake Heldings, who is the revolutionary scientist of the Modern Age and also the founder of the first-time machine. We can try and give him this gold because he has a huge lab, and did I mention that there is an archaeology department with him too? Well, we were packed and ready for the early morning flight back to Massachusetts, which I love. It must be snowing back there. I missed the Amazon, though. The tropical heat was really great, especially the unforgettable adventure that we had.

Back home!

The flight was as bad as the last. Not because I was sitting near another forest ranger but because the flight was turbulent. I didn't care a bit because I was so excited about the treasure. As soon as we got down, we sent Mom in a taxi home while me and dad took a ride to Jake's lab. As usual, we met Heldings under the trapdoor where we initially met him (it was a painful fall, mind you). As usual, we went to the workshop, where he seemed to be cooking something new. I didn't know what it was, but I definitely knew that we were going to test it any time soon. We quickly discussed everything with Heldings, who seemed to be getting excited at every moment. He quickly took the treasure and sent it to the Archaeological department. He said that most of the money from the museum would be for dad, whose eyes seemed to be gleaming. It had been a while since we heard from the Archaeological department. Jake said that the ornaments were from the ancient Mayan cities. I couldn't believe it for a moment. At school, everyone seemed to be murmuring as I passed through the entrance. I didn't know what the fuss was about, but I definitely knew that it had something to do with me. The only one who didn't murmur was Randy Fedro. He came towards me. For a second, I thought he was going to give me the boot for breaking his fence, but he didn't look so angry. In fact, he was excited. "Is that true that you found a treasure on Amazon all by yourself?" asked Randy. Before I could even begin my sentence, the whole school was swarming after me to know about my adventure. I was startled. How did these guys know about this news? When I thought about the news, it quickly hit me. Well, if this meant that I was one of the popular boys, then I should maintain this.

After having a blast in school by signing autographs for over 10,000 students, I believe I rushed back home. When I entered the heat of the drawing room, I felt exactly like I was in Amazon. There was a small envelope on the table. I took hold of it. On the back of the envelope, it was written that it was for me! I quickly rushed to Mom and asked if the letter was for me, and she quickly nodded. I rushed to my room and tore open the envelope to receive a letter. It went like this:

To:
James Tingly,
House No. 13, Phase_3,
Massachusetts,
United States of America.

Dear James,

You may know me from the flight. I am Thomas Rex, the real Thomas Rex, and I want to thank you for fulfilling my grandfather's dreams. I was the one who kept the map in that drawer. I forgot to lock it, though. My brother—you know him. He knocked me down on my way to the lodge, and he shut me up in the storeroom. I tried calling for help; the storeroom was near the playground, and no one came to my aid. Never mind; now I am happy, and it is all thanks to you, James.

Yours Truly,
Thomas Rex

I never knew that the real Thomas Rex was actually in the lodge itself! It was great to hear from him. But I still found out that the envelope wasn't empty, and I took out the remaining things. There was a bundle of money. Along with that, there was a pendent made of something that looked more like brass. I was really happy to receive all these as well as some pocket money. Behind the bundle of cash, there was a small slip, and it read, "Merry Christmas:)" Suddenly, there was the sound of dad calling me. I rushed down, and he was looking really satisfied. "Jake called me a few minutes before, and he told me that the research was complete and all these things were ancient Mayan. Well, hear the great news: the money we earn is 2 billion dollars as price money!" cried dad. I mean, he literally cried tears of joy. I think it was because we had some debt to clear. He suddenly hugged me, and it gave me a funny feeling. This was the feeling of family. Mom joined in as well. This was the family I knew.

The family that I loved Well, this was it—the end! We had a lot of cash in hand; we were famous; we cleared all our debts; what more could go wrong? I will meet you guys on another fantastic adventure. This is your beloved.

James Tingly!

www.ingramcontent.com/pod-product-compliance
Lightning Source LLC
LaVergne TN
LVHW061616070526
838199LV00078B/7300